SUPERHEROES
Don't Get Scared...

Or Do They?

By Zack Bush and Laurie Friedman. Illustrated by Sarah Van Evera.

Dedicated to you,
our wonderful reader—
a **SUPERHERO** in training.

Copyright © 2021 Publishing Power, LLC
All Rights Reserved
All inquiries about this book can be sent to the author at info@LittleSuperHero.com
Published in the United States by Publishing Power, LLC
ISBN: 978-1-7351130-8-1
For more information, visit our website: www.BooksByZackAndLaurie.com
Paperback

"We're just like real **SUPERHEROES**," said Ace.

"Yeah!" added Ava. "We're not scared of anything!"

Ace and Ava weren't even scared to swing so high that their **SUPERHERO** sneakers practically touched the clouds.

"We're not afraid of a storm!" said Ace.

Ava didn't say a word. She didn't like dark clouds. Or thunder. And especially not storms.

"Everyone gets scared," said Mom. "Even **SUPERHEROES**. They just know what to do when they feel afraid."

Ava listened carefully while Mom explained what she meant.

Ace was too busy doing his **SUPERHERO** exercises to hear a word she said.

Ava explained what Mom had told her.

"When **SUPERHEROES** get scared, they make sure they're safe. If they're not, they ask for help."

"What if they are safe?" asked Ace.

"Then they remind themselves that the thing that scares them can't really hurt them," said Ava.

Ace shined his **SUPERHERO** flashlight around the room. "Do you mean like the storm outside?"

"Exactly!" said Ava. "It's stormy outside, but we're safe inside."

That made Ace feel a little better. "Are there other **SUPERHERO** tricks?" he asked.

"Sure," said Ava. "When **SUPERHEROES** are scared, they take a deep breath. Then they close their eyes and count to ten so they stay calm."

"Staying calm helps you feel less scared?" asked Ace.

"Let's try it and see," suggested Ava. She and Ace took a deep breath. They closed their eyes and counted to ten.

They were busy counting when Mom came back into their room. "I thought I heard some little **SUPERHEROES**," she said.

Ace told Mom that Ava had told him what she'd said. "The **SUPERHERO** tricks worked!"

Mom smiled. "I'm glad," she said as she tucked Ace and Ava back into bed.

"The storm will end," she added, "and when you wake up in the morning, the sun will be out and shining."

Ace and Ava weren't exactly like the **SUPERHEROES** in their books. But . . . they were real **SUPERHEROES** who understood the power of knowing what to do when they were scared.

Mom even gave them badges to prove it.

CONGRATULATIONS!
You are a **SUPERHERO**
who knows what to do when you get scared!

Don't forget to go to the website
www.BooksByZackAndLaurie.com and print out your badge.
Keep reading all of the books in the #LittleSuperHeroSeries
to see all of the different ways that you can be a real superhero and earn more badges.
And if you like this book, please go to Amazon and leave a kind review.

Made in the USA
Middletown, DE
02 May 2021